I0783475

# The Fantastical Summer Forest Festival

### A Whimsical Bedtime Story

Author and Illustrator:
Katie Reed

Copyright © 2022 by Katie Reed
Text Copyright © 2022 by Katie Reed
Illustrations Copyright © 2022 Katie Reed

All rights reserved.


Independently Published

ISBN: 979-8-9868414-1-0

Author and Illustrator:

Katie Reed

Festival
A full moon rises,
As Spring fades away.
A warm breeze arrives,
Summer's on its way!

Lanterns hang on branches,
Strung low and high.
Glittering stars gather,
Twinkling in the sky.

Wisps appear on the path,
Their light all aglow.
They'll be your guides,
They know where to go...

The pixies arrive,
They hum a tune.
The stones are gleaming,
Enchanted by runes.

Bioluminescence,
Appears all around.
Moon-kissed soil,
Blankets the ground.

Woodland creatures,
Emerge from their homes.
Here come the griffins!
And old bearded gnomes!

Critters gather,
Circling around,
The Guardian Tree,
Ancient and brown.

The festival begins!
The old tree glows.
Its radiant light,
Puts on the first show.

The wisps join in,
They dance in sync.
Slow and graceful,
Then fade with a wink.

Sing Along:
Glowing light leads the way,
Into the night, out of day.
The brisk spring recedes,
Flowers rise from seed.
Come one, come all! Rejoice and Cheer!
The warmth of summer is finally here!

The pixies hum,
Then shift to song.
An upbeat tune,
Let's all sing along!

Moon berries plucked,
Laid neatly on plates,
Cheese and honey too!
The feast looks great!

Guests dance and eat,
The night is young.
Such lively music,
Great festival fun!

Lanterns twinkle,
To the beat.
While creatures dance,
And stomp their feet.

There's face painting, treats,
All sorts of games.
A dragon performs,
With magical flames!

MAGIC FIRE SHOW
SPECTACULAR

SHOW TIMES
9:00
10:00
11:00

BOB FOR APPLES

COTTON CANDY

Unicorns challenge griffins to race,
Across inky skies,
They tie...
For first place!

FINISH

The Forest Fest fills,
With laughter and delight.
A nocturnal party,
Awakens the night.

Balloon Darts
Bottle Toss

Popcorn
Bean Bag Toss

Firework
Show

Hours pass,
The music slows.
Bioluminescence,
Loses its glow.

The last event,
Is about to start.
The lantern ceremony;
Warms everyone's heart.

Star-bound lanterns,
Soar wishes away.
A sky full of dreams,
A magical display!

The stars grow weary,
The moon winks goodnight.
Sunrays peak out,
To offer their light.

Creatures grow sleepy,
And head home to rest.
Already dreaming,
Of the next Forest Fest.

Check out the **WIZARD AND THE LIZARD** series
written by Katie Reed and illustrations by Jenna Wing-Hu

Visit **katiereedauthor.com** for free crafts and coloring pages!

**Casting Kindness**
**Conjuring Confidence**
**Learning with Laughter**

www.ingramcontent.com/pod-product-compliance
Lightning Source LLC
Chambersburg PA
CBHW041417300726
48978CB00003B/133